This book belongs to:

....

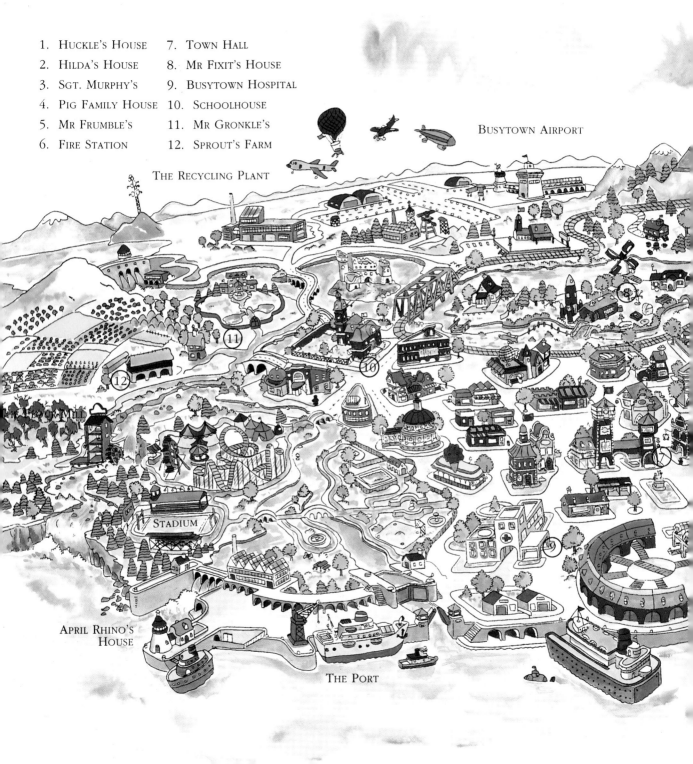

1. HUCKLE'S HOUSE
2. HILDA'S HOUSE
3. SGT. MURPHY'S
4. PIG FAMILY HOUSE
5. MR FRUMBLE'S
6. FIRE STATION
7. TOWN HALL
8. MR FIXIT'S HOUSE
9. BUSYTOWN HOSPITAL
10. SCHOOLHOUSE
11. MR GRONKLE'S
12. SPROUT'S FARM

THE RECYCLING PLANT

BUSYTOWN AIRPORT

STADIUM

APRIL RHINO'S
HOUSE

THE PORT

First published in Great Britain in 1995
by HarperCollins Publishers Ltd,
77-85 Fulham Palace Road,
Hammersmith, London W6 8JB
1 3 5 7 9 10 8 6 4 2
Copyright © 1995 The Estate of Richard Scarry
Adapted from the animated television series
The Busy World of Richard Scarry ™
produced by Paramount Pictures and Cinar
All rights reserved.
ISBN: 0 00 664572 0
Printed and bound in Italy
Designed and produced by Les Livres du Dragon d'Or

The Busy World of Richard Scarry

A Summer Picnic

Collins

An Imprint of HarperCollinsPublishers

The summer sun shines brightly on the river. By the mill the three old beggars, Wolfgang, Benny and Harry, are fishing.
"I just know we are going to catch something big today!" says Wolfgang.

Here comes the school bus bringing Miss Honey's class to the country for a picnic. It stops near the river bank. Miss Honey and the kids get out. "Are we are going to have our picnic here, Miss Honey?" Lowly asks. "Not here, Lowly, we need to go a little bit further up the river."

"Here's your picnic basket, Miss Honey," Spotty says. "Are you sure you don't want to come?" Miss Honey asks. "No thanks, I have to get back to school," Spotty replies. "Have fun everybody!"

Miss Honey has a special surprise for the children.
"We're going by boat to a beautiful place up the river!" she says.
"A boat! Hooray! Hooray!" cheer the children.
They put on life jackets, hop on board and begin to row.

"What a romantic place for a picnic!" says Hilda.
"Wow, Huckle!" Lowly exclaims. "Your mother made us an apple pie!"
"And I made some of my super–deluxe banana sandwiches with mayonnaise," Bananas says proudly.

"Miss Honey, I have just the thing for the sun!" says Hilda.
"What a handy rucksack you have, Hilda," Miss Honey remarks.

"I like to keep a few extra things for emergencies," Hilda explains. She pulls out a basketball, a football and a volleyball.

Look, Hilda's even brought a volleyball net! The children start to play.

Boom! Crack!
"What's that?" Kenny asks.

"Thunder and lightning," says Lynnie, trembling.

It starts to rain.

"Hurry up, children," Miss Honey calls. "We'll take shelter until the storm is over." She leads her class to the opening of a cave. "It should be nice and dry in here." "But it's so dark!" whimpers Lynnie, taking Miss Honey's hand.

Luckily, Hilda has some lanterns in her rucksack.

"Let's be explorers," suggests Huckle. "We can look for gold..."
"Or bananas!" adds Bananas Gorilla.

"I'll make the cave nice and cosy," Hilda
decides, "just in case we have to stay all night."
"All night! Oh no!" Sally moans.

"I brought this chair along, just in case," says Hilda. "Please have a seat, Miss Honey."

Poor Sally is still terrified. "Couldn't we just stand in the rain?" she asks. "I really don't mind getting wet." "Don't worry, Sally," Miss Honey says. "There's nobody here but us."

Deep inside the cave, the young explorers are at work. "Huckle, what are you looking for?" Billy Dog asks.

"Signs of cave men," says Huckle. "Look Huckle! Here are some ancient cave paintings," Lowly shouts. "But they are still wet," Billy Dog says. "Someone has just made these, or... someTHING!"

"Maybe we should go back," Huckle decides, "just in case."

They run back to join the others.

"Look! A monster! Help!"
Sally screams.
"Why Sally, it's only
Bananas' shadow," says
Miss Honey. "There are
no such things as monsters.
Can everybody please calm down?"

Billy Dog peers down
the dark tunnel.
"Huckle, if there's nobody
here but us, what are those
things?"

Six yellow eyes stare
out at them...

"Six yellow eyes!!!"
Billy Dog, Huckle
and Lowly all scream.

They race out of the
cave, followed by the
other children.

Miss Honey frowns at the children huddled under a tree.
"You are being very silly," she says. "There are no such thing as monsters. And I am going to prove it to you by going back inside!"

"Miss Honey, you can't go in there alone," says Huckle. "Lowly and I will come with you."

Miss Honey raises her lantern.
"You see?" she says. "There's nothing in here."

But suddenly, Lowly screams in horror.

"Look!" he shouts.

Lowly and Huckle rush out of the cave and join the other children under the tree.

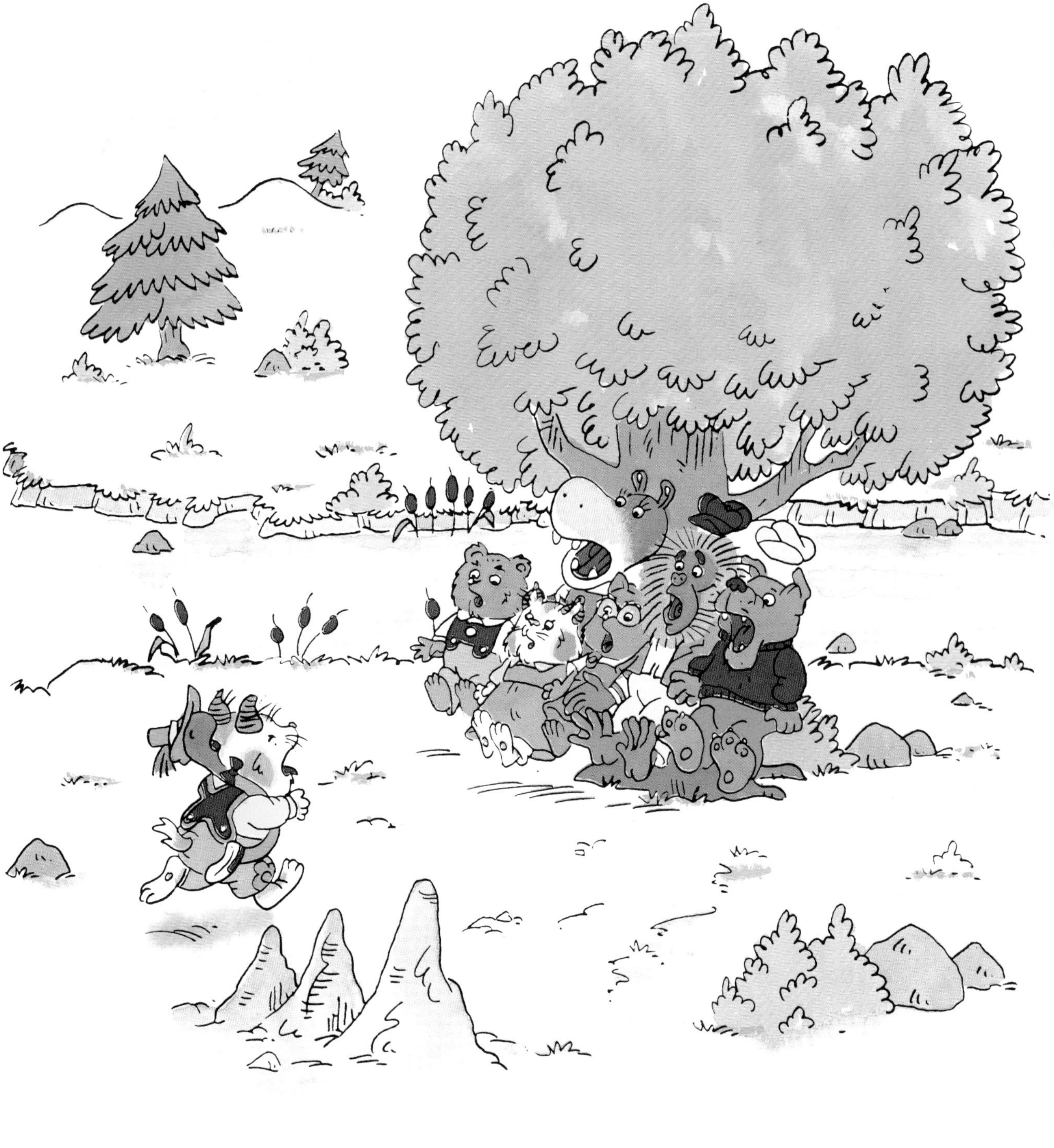

Soon Miss Honey comes out of the cave. "Look children, I've found your monster!"

"It was just Wolfgang, Benny and Harry. They went inside to get out of the rain too!" says Miss Honey.

"We thought all of YOU were monsters!" says Wolfgang.

"Well now that it's stopped raining, why don't you join our picnic?" suggests Miss Honey.

But the rainstorm has ruined the picnic – the boat is full of water and even the volleyball net is down!

Honk! Honk!
Here comes Spotty driving the school bus.

"It looks like you need a lift!" he says. "With the storm and everything, I thought you might need some help." Spotty drives them all to the beach.

"I'm afraid things didn't turn out quite the way I'd planned," says Miss Honey.

"Well," says Lowly, "sometimes the things you *don't* plan are the best fun of all!"

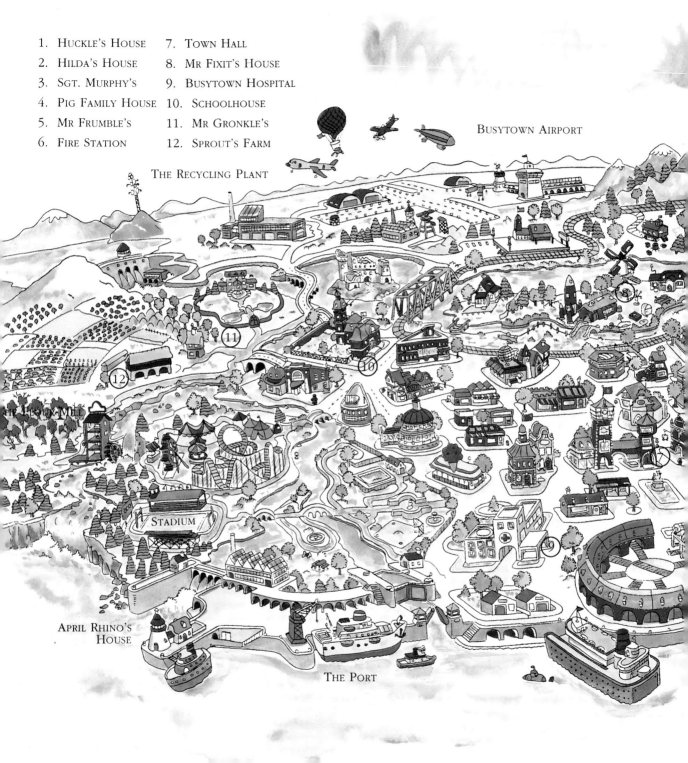

1. HUCKLE'S HOUSE
2. HILDA'S HOUSE
3. SGT. MURPHY'S
4. PIG FAMILY HOUSE
5. MR FRUMBLE'S
6. FIRE STATION
7. TOWN HALL
8. MR FIXIT'S HOUSE
9. BUSYTOWN HOSPITAL
10. SCHOOLHOUSE
11. MR GRONKLE'S
12. SPROUT'S FARM

THE RECYCLING PLANT

BUSYTOWN AIRPORT

STADIUM

APRIL RHINO'S
HOUSE

THE PORT

MOUNT BUSY OBSERVATORY

SKI CHALET

Welcome to Busytown!

CAMPING GROUNDS

BUSY BAY POINT

BRUNO'S SNACK STAND

THE BEACH

BUSYTOWN GRAND HOTEL

THE TRAIN STATION

SEA FORT